IN THE PALM OF MY HAND

Written by
JENNIFER RAUDENBUSH

Illustrated by
ISABELLA CONTI

RP|KIDS
PHILADELPHIA

For Art, who always offers a hand to hold, and for Evan
—J.R.

For my brave boys, Leo and Ale, for all the children,
this world is in your hands
—I.C.

Running Press Kids
Hachette Book Group
1290 Avenue of the Americas, New York, NY 10104
www.runningpress.com/rpkids
@RP_Kids

Printed in China

First Edition: March 2023

Published by Running Press Kids, an imprint of Perseus Books, LLC, a subsidiary of Hachette Book Group, Inc.
The Running Press Kids name and logo are trademarks of the Hachette Book Group.

The Hachette Speakers Bureau provides a wide range of authors for speaking events. To find out more,
go to www.hachettespeakersbureau.com or call (866) 376-6591.

The publisher is not responsible for websites (or their content) that are not owned by the publisher.

Print book cover and interior design by Frances J. Soo Ping Chow.

Library of Congress Control Number: 2021060374
Library of Congress Cataloging-in-Publication Data has been applied for.

ISBNs: 978-0-7624-7987-0 (hardcover), 978-0-7624-7988-7 (ebook),
978-0-7624-8018-0 (ebook), 978-0-7624-8019-7 (ebook)

APS

10 9 8 7 6 5 4 3 2 1

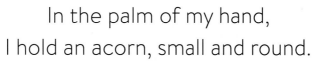

In the palm of my hand,
I hold an acorn, small and round.

Within it grows a forest.

And within that forest
towers an oak tree, tall and grand.

A caterpillar climbs its trunk.

In the palm of my hand,
I hold the caterpillar, fuzzy and plump.

Soon it will spin a cocoon and unfold its magic.

I follow a butterfly, airy and graceful.
It flutters and swoops, flutters and swoops,

guiding me on a flight of wonder.

In the palm of my hand,
I hold a wildflower, sweet and bright.

Within it blooms the seeds of forever-flowered fields.

I blow a meadow of wishes,
which whirl and twirl and swirl on the breeze,

floating toward a cloud, heavy and gray.

In the palm of my hand,
I hold a raindrop, cool and wet.

It has journeyed from the depths of the sea.

The wild ocean pushes and pulls, pushes and pulls toward land.
Its waves, salty and foaming,

tumble their treasures onto the shore.

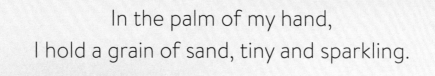

In the palm of my hand,
I hold a grain of sand, tiny and sparkling.

Within it lies a land of sandcastles.

As I build and mold,
a dreamy kingdom springs up,

calling me to adventures,
fantastic and bold.

In the palm of my hand,
I hold another hand, gentle and warm.

It gives a squeeze that hugs my heart.

Within the flickering firelight, I hold my family tight.
Love sparks and rises like smoke,

filling the world with love.

Now, in the palm of my sleepy hand,
I hold nothing . . . but it's not empty.

Like the star-speckled sky,
wide-open and limitless,

within me lives a universe of infinite possibilities.